The Story of Little Quack

To the young writers of Brandon School Division #40
B. G. & K. M. D.

Text copyright © 1990 by Betty Gibson
Illustrations copyright © 1990 by Kady MacDonald Denton

First U.S. Edition 1991

First published in Canada by Kids Can Press Ltd.

ISBN 0-316-30966-4

Library of Congress Catalog Card Number 90-53361
Library of Congress Cataloging-in-Publication information is available.

Joy Street Books are published by Little, Brown and Company (Inc.)

10 9 8 7 6 5 4 3 2 1

Printed in Hong Kong by Wing King Tong Co. Ltd

THE STORY of LITTLE QUACK

Written by Betty Gibson

Illustrated by Kady MacDonald Denton

Little, Brown and Company
Boston Toronto London

Jackie lived on a farm. He had a hen called Cluck and a dog named Woof. He had Buck the pony and a clumsy calf called Buttercup. But Jackie was lonesome.

Cluck was always busy laying eggs. Woof followed Jackie's father wherever he went. Buck galloped to the pasture every day, and Buttercup ran off with the other cows. No one stayed to play with Jackie.

One day, Jackie's mother brought him a duck.
"I'll call her Little Quack," said Jackie.
Little Quack was the perfect pet. She had plenty of time to play.

Every morning, when Jackie let the hens out into the yard, Little Quack followed him.

Every evening, when Jackie went to get the cows, Little Quack came, too. When Jackie went paddling in the pond, Little Quack swam beside him.

Jackie wasn't lonely anymore.
"You are my very best friend, Little Quack," said Jackie.

One day, Jackie and Little Quack went exploring.
Jackie took her to the barn to see the kittens and piglets
and lambs. He showed her Cluck and her yellow chicks.

Then they went to the pasture. Jackie showed
Little Quack where the lark had built her home.
He showed her the robin's nest on the maple branch,
and the hollow tree where a squirrel had a family.

They met Buttercup and Woof, but neither of them
paid attention to Little Quack.

One morning, Jackie couldn't find Little Quack. His mother helped him search, but they could not find Little Quack anywhere.

Jackie was very sad.

"I wonder if she went over the brook to Apple Hill Farm," said Jackie's father. "They have ducks there. Maybe Little Quack heard them when you walked with her in the pasture. Perhaps she is lonely."

"She couldn't be lonely," said Jackie. "I'm her friend, and I always play with her."

"Yes, but she might be lonely for other ducks just as you are sometimes lonely for other children."

Jackie and his father went to Apple Hill Farm.
And there she was!

Little Quack waddled over to Jackie and followed
him home.

The next morning Little Quack waited for Jackie on the doorstep. They worked and played together every day just as they used to.

One day, Little Quack disappeared again. This time she was not at Apple Hill Farm.

Jackie tried to play with the other animals. But Woof ran off after the tractor. Cluck had her chicks to guard, and Buttercup had grown too big to play.

A dozen times a day Jackie said, "Little Quack,
I wish you'd come home."

But a month went by and Jackie gave up hoping
she would return.

One day Jackie went to the far end of the pasture. He saw the lark's nest and chased a butterfly. He threw some corn to the gophers. Buttercup licked Jackie's hand and wandered off again. Buck tried to nibble Jackie's shirt and then ran away on his wobbly legs.

"I wish I had my duck," said Jackie.
Then he came to the brook.

There was Little Quack—and swimming with her were ten fluffy ducklings!

Little Quack came out of the water. Jackie fed Little
Quack some corn. The ducklings came out, too.
"Quack, quack, quack," they said.

How could he get Little Quack and her new family to the barnyard? Jackie wondered. Then he picked up the damp little ducklings and carried them home in his old felt hat.

"Look, Mommy," said Jackie. "I found Little Quack, and she has babies!"

"Little Quack won't be lonely now," said Jackie's father.

"I won't be lonely either," Jackie said, filling the old tub with water.

"Now I have Little Quack and her quacklings, too."